THIS WALKER BOOK BELONGS TO:

_____

_____

_____

First published 1988 by
Walker Books Ltd
87 Vauxhall Walk
London SE11 5HJ

This edition published 2007

4 6 8 10 9 7 5 3

Text © 1988 Sarah Hayes
Illustrations © 1988 Jan Ormerod

The right of Sarah Hayes and Jan Ormerod to be identified as author and
illustrator respectively of this work has been asserted by them in
accordance with the Copyright, Designs and Patents Act 1988

Printed in China

British Library Cataloguing in Publication Data:
a catalogue record for this book is
available from the British Library

ISBN 978-1-4063-0670-5

www.walkerbooks.co.uk

Eat up, Gemma

Sarah Hayes

illustrated by Jan Ormerod

WALKER BOOKS
AND SUBSIDIARIES

LONDON · BOSTON · SYDNEY · AUCKLAND

One morning we woke up late.
I couldn't find my shoes
and Gemma wouldn't eat her breakfast.
"Eat up, Gemma," said Mum,
but Gemma threw her breakfast on the floor.

Later on we went to the market.
Mum bought a bag of apples
and some bananas.
The man at the fruit stall
gave me a bunch of grapes.
He gave some to Gemma too.
"Eat up, Gemma," said the man,
but Gemma pulled the
grapes off one by one
and squashed them.

When we got home
Grandma had made the dinner.
"Nice and spicy," Dad said,
"just how I like it."
It was nice and spicy all right.
I drank three glasses of water.
"Eat up, Gemma," said Grandma.
Gemma banged her spoon on the table
and shouted.
But she didn't eat a thing.

The next day was Saturday
and Dad took us to the park.
We had chocolate biscuits for a treat.
I ate two and then another two.
"Eat up, Gemma," said Dad.
But Gemma didn't eat her biscuit.
She just licked off all the chocolate
and gave the rest to the birds.

In the evening our friends
were having a party.
"Eat up, everyone," said our friends.
And we did, all except Gemma.
She sat on Grandma's knee
and gave her dinner to the dog
when Grandma wasn't looking.

After the party my friend came to stay
and we had a midnight feast.
Gemma didn't have any.
She was too tired.

In the morning we made Gemma a feast.
"Eat up, Gemma," said my friend.
Gemma picked up her toy hammer
and banged her feast to pieces.
My friend thought it was funny,
but Mum and Dad didn't.

Soon it was time for us to put on
our best clothes and go to church.
I sang very loudly.

The lady in front of us
had a hat with fruit on it.
I could see Gemma looking and looking.

When everyone was really quiet
Gemma leaned forward.
"Eat up, Gemma," she said.

WALKER BOOKS is the world's leading

independent publisher of children's books.

Working with the best authors and illustrators

we create books for all ages, from babies

to teenagers – books your child will

grow up with and always remember. So…

FOR THE BEST CHILDREN'S BOOKS,
LOOK FOR THE BEAR

"Thank goodness for that," said Mum,
"We were getting worried," said Dad.
Grandma smiled at me.
I felt very proud.
"Gemma eat up," said Gemma,
and we all laughed.

"Eat up, Gemma," I said.
And she did.
She ate all the grapes
and the bananas.
She even tried to
eat the skins.

When we got home I had an idea.
I found a plate and a bowl.
I turned the bowl upside down
and put it on the plate.
Then I took a bunch of grapes
and two bananas and put them on the plate.
It looked just like the lady's hat.

Then she tried to pull
a grape off the lady's hat.
She pulled and pulled
and the lady's hat fell off.
Gemma hid her face in Dad's coat.